Pascual's Magic Pictures

Gage, Amy Glaser.
Pascual's magic pictures

c1996.
33305007344470
MI   04/07/97

Pascual's Magic Pictures

by Amy Glaser Gage

illustrated by Karen Dugan

Carolrhoda Books, Inc./Minneapolis

SANTA CLARA COUNTY LIBRARY

3 3305 00734 4470

To my family for their love and encouragement—A.G.G.
For Eliza Jane and Hope Marguerite Desmarais, with love from your friend Karen Dugan—K.D.

The author wishes to thank Rafael Salazar, Consul General of Guatemala, for his generous assistance in the preparation of this book.

Text copyright © 1996 by Amy Glaser Gage
Illustrations copyright © 1996 by Karen Dugan

All rights reserved. International copyright secured. No part of this book may be reproduced, stored in a retrieval system, or transmitted in any form or by any means, electronic, mechanical, photocopying, recording, or otherwise, without the prior written permission of Carolrhoda Books, Inc., except for the inclusion of brief quotations in an acknowledged review.

Carolrhoda Books, Inc. c/o The Lerner Group
241 First Avenue North, Minneapolis, MN 55401

Library of Congress Cataloging-in-Publication Data

Gage, Amy Glaser.
    Pascual's magic pictures / by Amy Glaser Gage ; illustrations by Karen Dugan.
        p.   cm.
    Summary: Having saved enough money to buy a disposable camera, Pascual goes into the Guatemalan jungle to take pictures of monkeys, but the results are not what he expected.
    ISBN 0-87614-877-1
    [1. Photography—Fiction. 2. Monkeys—Fiction. 3. Guatemalan—Fiction.] I. Dugan, Karen, ill. II. Title.
PZ7.G1216Pas   1996
[E]—dc20   95-22331

Manufactured in the United States of America
1 2 3 4 5 6 – JR – 01 00 99 98 97 96

Pascual looked up into the trees.

"I wish I had a camera," he said to himself as he watched a baby howler monkey jump from branch to branch above his head.

In one swoop, the monkey snatched Pascual's hat and dove onto a dog's back. The dog turned its head and snapped, but the monkey was too quick. It leaped from the dog and grabbed a blanket lying on the ground.

"Scat, you crazy monkey!" a merchant yelled.

The monkey pulled the blanket. Colorful weavings, wood carvings, and beads scattered across the road.

Pascual fell to the ground laughing as the monkey disappeared with his hat into the Tikal jungle.

"Excuse me," a woman said, interrupting Pascual's laughter.
Pascual looked up into a friendly face. "Do you like?" he
asked, practicing his English. He pointed to the shirts he was
selling.

"Yes, very much," replied the woman.

"Sixty *quetzales* for two," Pascual said quickly. The woman
offered forty *quetzales,* and they settled on fifty.

"Hey, can I take your picture?" she asked.

Pascual stared at her camera. It was different from any camera he'd ever seen. It was small and yellow and looked like it was made out of cardboard. It hung from her neck by a string.

"That's a camera?" asked Pascual.

"It's a disposable camera," the woman replied. "You take twelve pictures with it and then throw it away."

"Throw it away?!"

She explained. "When you're done, you send the whole camera to this company." She pointed to some words on the box. "They develop the pictures and send them back to you. I guess they throw the camera away."

"How much it costs?"

"About ten dollars," the woman said. "Let's see . . . five *quetzales* to a dollar . . . that's . . . "

"Fifty *quetzales*," blurted Pascual.

The woman smiled and handed Pascual five *quetzales*. "To help you save for a camera," she explained.

"*Gracias.* Thank you! *!Que Dios se lo pague!*" said Pascual as he grinned for the picture.

That evening, Pascual met up with his brother and father, who had been working in nearby fields. They took turns pushing the oxcart as they walked home. After supper, they counted the day's earnings.

"There's a little more," said Pascual. He held out the crinkled bill that the woman had given him.

"You keep that," his father said. "You've earned it."

Pascual thanked his father and stuffed the bill back in his pocket. "I'm going to save to buy a camera," he said proudly.

"What for?" asked his brother, Tomás.

"I want to take pictures of monkeys."

Tomás laughed. "It'll take you years to save up enough for a camera," he said. "It's better to spend your money now on Coca-Cola and candies."

"You'll see," said Pascual.

On Saturdays, Pascual was the first merchant to set up along the road outside Tikal, and the last one to pack up. And every Saturday night, Pascual put the tips he earned in a little bag that he wore around his neck. Each week, as the bag got heavier, so did his longing for a camera.

"I've saved enough money to buy a camera," Pascual
announced one evening. He told his family about the
disposable camera.

"Papa, will you take me to Guatemala City to buy one?"

"It's a very long trip," his father answered. "But I'll take you
with me to get supplies next month. We'll stay with our
cousins."

When the day of the trip arrived, Pascual shook his father awake. They walked to the bus stop beneath a mango-colored sky. Pascual shared a seat with two peasant women. One woman held a baby wrapped in a shawl. Pascual's father stood in the aisle. Every time they hit a bump, Pascual's head bobbed, his father stumbled, and the baby wailed. Several bumpy hours passed before they reached a paved road.

At dusk, Pascual and his father stepped off the bus on a quiet street just outside Guatemala City. Wearily, they walked to their cousins' home.

The next morning, they thanked their cousins with cacao seeds that they had brought from the fields near Tikal. "Make lots of chocolate!" Pascual called out over his shoulder as they said their good-byes. Then he and his father walked to the heart of Guatemala City.

Pascual squeezed his father's hand. He had never seen so
many things moving so fast nor heard so much noise—the
roaring of cars, buses, and motorcycles, the blaring of horns,
and the calls of street vendors. They walked quickly past the
vendors selling *pan dulce*—sweet bread—and *sandía*—
watermelon juice. Pascual knew he had only enough money
to buy a camera.

When they finally found a camera store, Pascual immediately selected a yellow camera, just like the one he had seen hanging around the woman's neck.

"I bet that won't take good pictures," said Tomás when Pascual showed him the camera.

"Yes, it will," said Pascual.

"Why do you think all those tourists have those fancy cameras?" said Tomás. "They can take pictures of the fleas on a monkey's back. Your camera won't do that."

"You'll see," said Pascual.

"I want to take my pictures inside the Tikal jungle," Pascual told his father.

"Okay," his father said. "But be careful of the jaguar. When you're in the jungle, you're in *his* territory."

The moment he entered the park, Pascual understood why his father had told him to be careful. The jungle was dark, and there were strange noises. When he finally stopped at the stone ruins of a palace, his body tingled with excitement. He felt magic all around him.

Pascual pulled his camera out of his bag and set it beside him. Then he leaned against a stone slab and looked up at the treetops.

Suddenly, a roar sent his heart into his throat. It had to be a jaguar! He leaped up and ran, slowing only as he remembered his father's warning. *"You should never turn your back on a jaguar. If you face the jaguar, it won't attack."*

"I never should have run," Pascual said aloud. "I could have been hurt. And I left my camera, too."

Pascual knew he had to go back. He clenched his fists and took a deep breath. Then he turned around and began to walk back.

Soon he came to the stone slab he had leaned against. But his camera was nowhere to be found.

Just then, a roar pierced the jungle. It was deep and powerful—and familiar. And suddenly Pascual knew. He had run, not from a jaguar, but from a family of howler monkeys— the very animals he had come to photograph!

Pascual slumped to the ground and buried his head in his hands. From the tree above him, the howlers roared and threw sticks and twigs at him.

After a while, the monkeys swung to a neighboring tree, and Pascual lifted his head. Then he put his hands on the ground to push himself up.

"What is this?" he said, lifting one hand to look beneath it. His mouth fell open. "I knew this was a magic spot!"

Pascual grabbed his camera and hugged it to his chest.
Then he brought it up to his eyes and skimmed the treetops
for the monkeys. They were gone.

My first picture will be of this place, thought Pascual. To
remind me not to fear the howlers' roar.

He aimed the camera and pressed the button. Nothing happened. He tried again.

"You're broken!" he shouted at the camera. Then he noticed the word *End* in the camera's window. All twelve pictures were used up, yet he hadn't taken a single one.

Angrily, Pascual stuffed the camera back in his bag and started home. All the way home, he thought about his camera and what he would tell his family. Finally, he decided to tell them nothing. He would send the camera off and wait.

Every week for six weeks, Pascual ran to the post office in nearby Santa Elena. And every week, the postmaster shook his head. Finally the postmaster smiled and handed him a thick envelope. The pictures had come.

"What's in your hand?" Tomás asked when Pascual got home.

"My pictures."

"Come on. Open them!" Tomás demanded.

Pascual's mother and father ran into the room.

"I'd like to open them by myself," Pascual said. He knelt on his sleeping mat facing the corner and tore open the envelope.

"Well? How are they?" said Tomás.

Pascual was silent for a long time. So long, in fact, that even his brother looked worried. "Well?"

"They're . . . wonderful," said Pascual.

"Let's see!" said Tomás, grabbing the pictures.

"Wonderful," echoed Pascual's mother and father.

"Wow!" whispered Tomás. "But I only count eleven. You must be hiding one."

Pascual placed the final picture in front of his family.

Tomás's mouth dropped open. "How'd you take that picture?"

Pascual smiled.

"Magic," he said.